Mr. Dortle's

four kids save the world

ISBN 978-1-95081-811-2 (paperback)

Rushmore Press LLC
1 888 733 9607
www.rushmorepress.com

Printed in the United States of America

Mr. Dortle's
four kids save the world

MAME YAA

Chapter One

Once upon a time, there lived Mr. Dortle and his four bratty boys. They lived in the secluded part of the neighborhood in a developing town which consist of many trees and filled with lots of wonder. In this green vegetated neighborhood there is a hidden forest at the outskirt of the town which comes alive every afternoon and this is where the four boys always find themselves.

The thick trees and the strong earthy smell bring in the feel of a welcoming atmosphere; but the cunning character of the forest is hidden behind the cloud of smile that it brings to its visitors. This forest has had quite a number of visitors but none of them ever came back, whether they were alive or not is still a mystery.

The untouched branches stretches across the skies and give the forest a blanket pattern of blue green and white feel. For a time now the rain has taken charge bringing out the freshness of the entire forest and giving way for the thick fog and the sunlight penetrate through to set in. The v-shaped pond adds a special appeal to the forest. Now you would think this forest consist of only wild animals, but there are no wild ones except for the grass eating ones. The forest is the opposite of itself making it a pleasant place for the boys to play. Anyone in the neighborhood who had ever gone there and come back discouraged others from ever entering that cunning forest. But to Mr. Dortle's boys it is the safest place they could ever be.

Chapter Two

One hot afternoon something frightening and mysterious was filled in the air. Nothing was done in its regular order; some of the natives of the land had gone missing everyone going about their normal duties did so this afternoon with much fright. The boys wondered what happened; papa, papa, they came shouting from the mouth of the forest towards their brick hut Burtle; the eldest entered and searched thoroughly through the house but their father was missing. Jodle; the third born joined in, where is papa he shouted with much scare in his Voice. He's gone Eddle the second born said. Mettle the fourth; broke down into tears and the rest joined in. How are we going to find him; Mettle finally spoke with tears in his eyes. The rest joined him and they hugged themselves finding comfort from each other. Suddenly, Jodle pulled back; I think I know where papa is. Where! They all shouted simultaneously looking confused at him. In the forest he said.

He pointed at the direction. How sure are you Eddle asked? I am very sure sounding confident; look at those footsteps they belong to papa. They all turned and looked at it. Now sure of where their father was they prepared themselves to enter the forest to look for him. They followed the footsteps until it stopped. Where is papa and where do you think he would be? One of them asked they began feeling very lonely since their father was their friend. They do not have many good friends in the village and it is only their father who truly knew them and kept encouraging them that they would do great things.

They continued into the forest with a gloomy feel in the atmosphere.

As they walked through the forest, a tensed feel in the air clothed itself around them and looking ahead of them they saw something move. Each held the hand of the other as they have never been to this part of the forest. They were frightened each wondering what that was and if their father was safe. A wind was rising and making a singular wild, low rushing sound. But it was not the sea; it was lots of gathered wind blowing through the forest. It rushed by and whistled and made strange sounds along the path they went on making it tiresome walking freely. They heard a great deal of rushing water moving very fast with a great deal of noise but they could not make out where it was coming from.

Chapter Three

I don't like it Eddle whispered to himself but the others heard it. What did you say one of them asked? I don't like this feeling he repeated pinching his lips tightly together. They walked round and round in circles and always came back to the same spot. Look it is the same tree again we walked by this tree and we have come back to the same spot; Jodle said. You are right, Burtle pointed, look! My pouch; I guess it fell when we walked by earlier on. As they walked on they saw an old man with a spade on his shoulders he seemed not to be bothered by them. He just whistled and walked on. The boys were startled wondering what an old man would be doing in the forest alone.

"What is this place"; Eddle shouted. They looked around and realized they were in a cemetery. A chilly wind began blowing around them. When did we get here they wondered. It is strange something about this forest has changed. There were strange red birds with large eyes and talons hovering on the graves and the leafless trees that surrounded it. Something else was filled in the air. Voices echoing from afar but nobody could be seen. At this point the boys were frightened.

Listen there is someone crying where is it coming from? The woods shouted Mettle's name. It seems to be getting closer. Run guys run. And at that very moment a grave door opened for a great wind rushed through the forest following through the passage they were running. It followed from behind lifting and tossing everything it came across. It lifted the boys and blew them to the other side of the forest. The rain was pouring heavily on this side of the forest and the trees and shrubs were almost hidden by a gray mist and cloud. They could hardly see the grounds they stood on except for strong smell of dark red sand and the grass smells.

They felt perplexed. Suddenly the old man with spade appeared; he seemed to be digging into the soil and pushing the soil to the side.

Hello! Jodle said, sir we are lost and we are seeking for your help.

He stopped digging and answered, what help do you need; he said in his grumbling Voice, and quite suddenly he seemed to get angry with them, though they did not see why he should.

Now look here! He said sharply. What are you doing here this is not a place you young boys should be. It is dangerous out here.

Just about that moment a rabbit came hopping around, it seemed to be chasing after something. Look here the old man said, this is not actually a rabbit but something else.

The boys were astonished at his words because what they are seeing with their eyes is a rabbit. As the old man disappeared the rabbit changed into a boy holding a rough wooden pipe. He was a funny looking boy about ten wearing a funny smile across his lips. He looked very clean though and his nose turned up and his cheeks looked as red as poppies. He started playing his pipe ignoring the boys who were watching him in fright and amazement. The strange low little sound his pipe seemed to make attracted birds and rabbits near. When he finally stopped playing his pipe he held up his hand and spoke to them in a Voice a little higher than the sound from his pipe.

Don't you move, the boys remained motionless until whatever was behind them had passed by.

Chapter Four

My name is mezelwart and I am the keeper of the forest. The thing behind you was one of the wicked shadows that linger around looking for ignorant souls like you. He smiled at them as a form of welcoming them into his forest.

I know you need my help and I am willing to give it. You are seeking for your father and the others. At this point the boys were completely startled. How did you know? they asked rather curiously. I know because I have seen them; I could not help them because it was not my territory. So how do we find them especially our father? Mettle asked. I can take you there. What are you waiting for then they spoke together as though it was rehearsed. You need to rest first. We don't need rest we demand to see him immediately. You don't know what you ask boys he said. You said you will take us there. He walked back and forth with his pointing finger which had long nails in his mouth and biting on it as though that was where his thoughts were. He turned around sharply giving them an intense gaze. With his eyes widely opened and his mouth a little pouted. He then dropped his gaze and smile spread across his face. Of course I will take you he said. But are you prepared? He said as he vanished onto a tree branch and sat on it. Prepared for what? They sounded confused. The sacrifice, he said, looking down at them. What sacrifice, they asked looking up at him.

Before you can take someone back he said; the spirits demand a sacrifice. The boys looked at each other astonish and then back at him. But he had disappeared to the top of the tree. He sat on the tree branch with his left knee supporting his jaw and his other leg hanging loosely swinging back and forth. Look! Over there is a house you could go and rest for there is a long journey ahead of you.

Chapter Five

A man with high rather crooked shoulders who wore a long black hair streaked with white turned over his shoulders to speak to them; come closer he said. He was not ugly as they had assumed. He rubbed his forehead fretfully as he spoke to them. What brings you young boys here? With his soft old Voice he muttered something absentmindedly.

Excuse us for our intrusion sir; but we needed a place to rest. A strange sound came from the man's throat which frightened them. They moved back; with the thought of running at any instant. Noticing their hesitation; don't be frightened, he said in a worried Voice. I am just too sick and wretched and distracted but I'll still help you.

They heard a faint sound of fretful crying which came in a distance. They listened for a few minute until it faded, this frightened them the more. Take this; it's my teardrop when you need it splash the tear on the ground and I will come to your aid. Thank you sir they replied.

They journeyed as fast as they can deep into the forest, look over there on that tree there is mezelwart; Jodle pointed. Mezelwart appeared and gave them a wide curvy smile. I am here to help and to lead you since I am the keeper of the forest. They felt protected as they thought a demi god was on their side. They walked on to a dark foggy area where nothing could be felt or seen except the bitter taste of the fog. They held each other's hand to avoid losing the other. Mezelwart changed form into a white attired man and spoke an unknown tongue, the fog cleared and to the boys amazement they were suspended in the air above ground level. It felt funny and frightful. Still holding each other's hand, mezelwart held unto their clothes and landed them safely on the ground. They realized they were at a section of the forest they never imagine existed. It was filled with dry and hungry skinny trees pleading for water from the dry ground which they stood on. Dead carcasses of animal bones and rotten leaves filled the air with an unpleasant smell. The dense air produced less sufficient oxygen for breathing. The dark earthy ashes felt moist making it difficult to walk through. There was really nothing exciting to see. What happened here? Burtle asked. This is where you call ghost town where the souls are found. But you can't see anything here, Mettle said. Open your eyes and you will see. They strained had to see but still could not see anything. Mezelwart chuckled and shook his head; he waved his hand in their faces as if to remove something. I see something one of them exclaimed. Me too another said. Jodle began crying because he could not see anything. Mezelwart looked at the poor soul with much compassion and thinking of a way to help him; what do you have in your hand; he asked. It the tear drops. Yes the tear drop. Hand it over.

Chapter Six

Jodle gave it to mezelwart who opened it and put some on jodle's eyes and splashed the rest on the ground suddenly a thick smoke appeared as when a genie would appear and disappeared before their eyes. What's that? They turned to look at the direction of his pointed finger. They saw a familiar face but this time a handsome and more energetic man approaching them. It is you Jodle said. Yes it is me. I promised you when you need my help I will come to your aid. You can see now Jodle; mezelwart said. Of course I can; sounding happier than the worries that lie ahead. Can you see all these people walking around us? Jodle asked. Which people? Eddle jumped with fear looking about him to find anything odd. Well, the familiar man said because he has my teardrop in his eyes he can see beyond what the forest allows you to see. The boys looked up at him thinking of what he said. We need to hurry if we want to catch up with what is going on, on the other side. Mezelwart cut in. the boys agreed. But where do we go from here; Jodle asked.

The familiar man spoke something and two large leaves with the shape of a surfer's board appeared. Wow! You want us to climb on that Mettle asked. No way; that is so cool, Jodle with much enthusiasm climbed on and the rest had no choice but to do the same. Fly; fly away to the very place we want to be. The leaves carried them high above so that they could see the top of the trees. The forest was amazing but this place in particular was very awful. No green trees or flowers. Just grey ashes of even stones.

As frightened as the boys were, they took time to enjoy the moments high up searching everywhere to see if they could see their small hut. Finally the leaves stopped and started dropping with great speed but to their surprise something held on to their feet gripping them firmly to the surface of the leaf. They realized mezelwart had made the veins of the leaf wrap itself to their feet. They felt quite insecure and yet they knew they would not fall.

As soon as they landed on the ground the veins unwrapped itself and disappeared just as it came. They walked through the thick fog in silence. The only sounds that could be heard were frog sounds, crashing leaves and strange weird cries coming from the deeper side of the forest. As they walked further hey began to see trees with strange face marks and strange faces like stones. They felt the tension in the air feeling each other's warm breath in their faces and ears. It was then they realized they have come to the deadly place where the souls disappeared to. Each time they walked on further, they heard strange moans and sorrowful cries behind them. Sometimes they get frightened as they encounter stranger things.

Stand still and be quiet Jodle said to the rest of them; there is something hovering and moving around us.

Chapter Seven

For a minute, they stood quietly in a motionless manner. It's gone he said. They released the air they've been holding in. What was that? Mettle asked. It was one of those wicked spirits trying to smell for human souls. But why did it leave, Mettle asked again. I repelled it with my scent; they don't like green leafy scents like mine and mezelwart. Yet still there are some that will try to harm us when given the chance that was why we all froze together to avoid any distractions. As they got closer to the cave they to heard noises of people crying for help. Here is it, the cave of souls; mezelwart whispered. They crept slowly and quietly as they can and hid behind a large stone hill. It was big enough to hide behind. Slowly they lifted their heads to look at what was going on. The souls were enslaved, chained together and put to hard work. Their slave masters were on them watching their every move and not leaving their sight for a second. Look on the other side what are those things bound together. Mezelwart looked at them worriedly zooming closer with his mind to have a close look, he said with deep pain in his Voice; they are the bodies of the soul; they are chained together so that the souls cannot escape. Is there a way out, Eddle asked with much concern thinking of the last memory shared with his father. But how can we help them? Jodle asked curiously. You; my dear boy are the answer; you would have to sacrifice yourself. No,

never, how can we sacrifice our brother, the three spoke simultaneously. Our father loves us very much but his love for Jodle is very deep, he always believed Jodle was meant for greatness so even if we manage to save our father he would still not be happy knowing what has happened to him. Perhaps, the familiar man said, this is the greatness your father was talking about.

Hush everybody! Mezelwart whispered. Something is coming our way. Mezelwart disappeared from amongst them to search for a way through the cave. Come on signaling with his hand, this way. Come on, we would shield you, he whispered. They hurriedly followed him trying as much as they can to avoid being seen. They almost got away except for the last door where their captain is. He had the ability to see beyond their covering. Catch them they are getting away. He pointed his greyish staff at them and a force from the staff lifted the ball covering from over them exposing them naked to the rest of them. They drew their words and whip. The boys felt frightened and intimidated at first but they gathered up courage to fight the monsters off. The monsters drew their swords to strike them but the familiar man counteracted with a white smoke which filled the air and preventing them from moving towards them they rushed towards them and pushed them down to floor. Each time the monsters touched the floor they vanished into thin air and multiplied. Jodle's second eye which is the invisible eye that sees beyond what the normal eyes can see opened. This gave him the power to direct the others on what to do. Whatever you do, don't make them touch the ground. It is better they die in the air than falling on the ground alive. The familiar man spoke some unknown words and a thick fog surrounded them giving a covering so they could move easily and closer to their predators. Mezelwart spoke and the tree vines came crawling through. Attack! He shouted. The vines and hugh roots grabbed the monsters wrapped themselves around them and choke the life out of them. The captain of the monsters also shouted to the others do not give up don't allow this little dwarfs to overtake you. They fought until the monsters were just a hand full. The captain laughed at them, whatever you do you still can't get out alive; he said. They had fought their through to the last place where the sacrifice was to be made. The captain and his men stood guard to prevent it from happening. Unaware, a huge root hit them hard giving them a great fall on the ground and rendering some of them unconscious. The captain looked on while Jodle run into the path and went deep inside it. Suddenly, the captain gave a big shout and broke into pieces like the struck of lightening. The freed souls went into their bodies and the chains broken. They rose up looking at each other and it was a vast Number of people. Mezelwart limped on his broken leg to meet the rest. The three boys wore a sad face because of their lost brother. As they gathered around searching for family members, friends and their dad, a loud noise shook the ground and all were terrified. Two people approached them in a shadow-like manner, at first their heights were the same until they came closer. All started rejoicing because Jodle and his father were alive.

CPSIA information can be obtained
at www.ICGtesting.com
Printed in the USA
BVHW021054030919
557357BV00008BA/205/P

9 781950 818112